AF429783

MAX WALKER
PAST DUE

Michael Gerhardt

&

Roger Meyers

This is a work of fiction. Names, characters, places and incidents are the product of the author's imagination, or are used fictitiously. Any resemblance to actual events, locales or persons, living or dead, is coincidental.

Copyright 2020

All rights reserved. No part of this publication may be produced, distributed or transmitted in any form or by any means, or stored in a database or a retrieval system, without the written permission of the publisher.

DIAMOND PUBLISHING

First Edition: 2020

10 9 8 7 6 5 4 3 2 1

ISBN: 9798563465947

BOOKS IN THE MAX WALKER SERIES:

THE ABYSS

THE TIGHTROPE

BREAKING EVEN

BREAKING THROUGH

THE CONFRONTATION

PAST DUE

BOOKS IN THE LORI NICHOLS SERIES

SPYMISTRESS

RANSOM

FRENCH LACE

SINGAPORE PEARL

COBRAS OF INDIA

ROAD TO DESPAIR

WAGES OF SIN

THE CAIRO CONNECTION

WATER OVER THE DAM

GOING TWICE

ALSO BY MICHAEL GERHARDT

PRESIDENTIAL POWERS

THE LINCOLN AFFAIR

THE RODINA PLOT

BLACK PAWN

THE INCREDIBLE COUSINS AND THE MAGIC CABOOSE

MISS KITTY & THE KRACKERKNOCKER

ALSO BY ROGER MEYERS

BEDTIME STORIES

HOW TO WIN – LISTEN

LIFE ENHANCEMENT

THE LAST SQUIRREL

UNION MADE

ARTICLES OF LOVE

PROLOGUE

This book is the sixth book in the **Max Walker** series. In case you did not read the previous books, we have provided a very brief summary of the story line in order for you to understand what is happening in this particular book.

Max Walker is a foreman on a production line in an automobile plant in Ohio. His daughter, Charlotte is a student at Stanford University and his son, Steven, dropped out of high school and ran away from home almost two years before the story begins.

On their twenty-fifth wedding anniversary Max took his wife, Claire, to New York City. While having lunch at an outdoor setting in Times Square, a terrorist attack occurred and Max and Claire fled the scene. During the action, Claire was killed, and Max felt it was his fault. After recovering from his own injuries, he spent time in the home of his sister in law and her family in Connecticut. In an effort to return meaning to his life, He agreed to accompany his nephew on his journey back to school in Florida.

 At the urging of his nephew, Max purchased a used motor home with the plan to travel cross country to visit his daughter in California. He first visits Key West, where he gets involved in a dive for treasure on a 400 hundred year old sunken Spanish ship. His companions turn out to be criminals and he manages to escape with his life and a jar of emeralds.

On his way to New Orleans, he picks up a hitch hiker named Drew, a young physics student from New York. When they reach New Orleans, Max discovers that his son, Steven, is in jail, to be tried as an accessory to murder. Max uses some of the emeralds from the dive in Key West to raise money, and, with Drew's help, he is able to obtain Steven's release, but his son still refuses to see him.

Steven gets a job working on a ship searching for oil in the Gulf, and Max goes to Galveston to meet the ship when it docks at the end of its mission. On the way he stops in Houston and is involved in a mall shooting. Steven survives a hurricane in the Gulf but is injured and hospitalized when he reaches Galveston. Max finally meets with Steven and they begin the healing process.

But the two characters from the dive in Florida show up and want Max's emeralds, and he enlists Drew's help to execute a plan to get rid of their threat once and for all. This brings you up to date. We hope you enjoy this episode and, if you missed them, go back to read the first five!

CHAPTER 1

HOTEL DINING ROOM

GALVESTON, TEXAS

Max was sitting across from Marcia Fullbright, a woman who he had come into frequent contact with lately. He enjoyed looking at her face, a classic beauty to say the least. And she was bright, talented, extremely successful and rich. He clearly liked being with her, but his still damaged psyche couldn't get past the fact that he had lost Claire, his wife of twenty-five years only a few short months ago. But, in that time, Marcia had helped him rescue his son, Steven from a serious criminal charge, gotten Steven a job that had led to the beginnings of a reconciliation between he and Steven, and helped him get rid of a couple of very nasty characters who were bent on doing him personal harm.

His attention snapped back to the present as he realized she was talking to him.

"So, what's next?" Marcia asked.

He shrugged.

"I don't know for sure. Steven is out of the hospital. He's leaving tomorrow on the *Eureka* on another job for one of your companies." He paused and shrugged again, not sure where to go next. She helped him out.

"And I'm leaving for Europe. I'm speaking at a convention of scientists in Oslo."

"Oh? What about?"

"The meetings are all about global warming and what to do about it. I'm talking about what we're learning during our explorations in the Gulf of Mexico."

"Ah!" he said.

"Ever been there?" she asked

He glanced out the window at the beach and water, not sure what she meant. She saw his glance and smiled.

"Sorry. I meant Oslo, not the Gulf of Mexico."

"Oh," he said and smiled. "No, never been there."

"Beautiful city. In fact, a beautiful country." She paused before continuing. "Care to come along?"

Max was surprised by the question. He thought a moment before answering.

"I'd love to."

Marcia sensed his hesitation.

"But?"

"I've got some unfinished business here. I really need to get to California to see my daughter."

"I could fly her here when we return. In fact, bring her along to Oslo."

Max just stared at her. She was a truly remarkable woman and she was trying hard. It was very flattering on the one hand, but somewhat bewildering on the other. She could have any man she wanted. What did she see in him? He hesitated so long that Marcia began squinting at him.

"Max?"

"I'm sorry, Marcia. This isn't really fair to you. But I've got to get my head back on straight, you know?

She forced a tight smile.

"Of course."

The palpable silence began to push them apart, and Max fought to dispel it.

"When do you get back?" he asked. "Maybe I'll be done by then."

She took a deep breath before answering.

"One can only hope, right?"

She raised her right hand a few inches and the waiter instantly appeared.

"Johnathan. I'll be leaving now. Mister Walker will be remaining here at the table for a while. Put everything on my tab, please."

"Of course, Miss Fullbright."

She stood and reached out her hand toward Max.

"I hope you are able to right your ship, Max. I wish you all the best."

Max stood and took her hand. It was warm and she had a strong grip.

"I'm sorry, Marcia. Can I call you when," he paused, not sure what end point to put on his current struggles.

"When you feel you are ready, please do, Max."

She extracted her hand and swiftly and smoothly left the restaurant. Max watched her go, wondering if he would ever see her again.

"I hope so," said out loud and sat back down at the table.

CHAPTER 2

A DOCKSIDE DINER

GALVESTON, TEXAS

Max rubbed his eyes and swallowed another shot from his second cup of coffee, trying to wake up. The call from Steven had come at four AM asking him if he wanted to meet for a quick bite. Captain Wahl had decided that six AM this morning was the perfect time to set sail, and he wanted all hands on board by five AM. Max shook his head again just as Steven dashed through the door. He spotted Max and hurried over.

"Sorry, Dad. Had no control over the timing," he said as he pulled the chair out and sat. The waitress arrived immediately, obviously aware of the time crunch of a soon to depart ship. Steven ordered coffee but no food.

"Not hungry?" Max asked, and Steven shook his head.

"There'll be plenty of food on board."

They stared at each other for a moment and Max broke the ice.

"This seems like a great opportunity you've come up with." Steven nodded.

"It's awesome. Captain Wahl says that I have a good head for the job. He gave me some charts and an app for learning how to read them, and has been impressed how quickly I've learned."

A small pang of jealousy stabbed at Max's chest, but he hid it.

"Gee, that's great."

"Yeah. It's the first time," Steven started and quickly stopped himself. Max sensed they were approaching the subject of why Steven had left home.

"First time what, buddy?" Max prompted, using the nickname he had called Steven as a child. Steven colored a little at the sound of the name.

"Well, the first time I've felt like I was good at something, anything really."

Max sat for a moment, processing the information before replying.

"Is that why you left? You felt I thought you were no good at anything?"

Steven shrugged as the waitress delivered his coffee.

"Well, you were right. I'm not a good athlete, and I'm certainly not smart like Charlotte. And I don't have any interest in cars like you do."

He pulled the cup to his lips and drank, leaving the conversation ball in Max's court.

"But," Max began, and then stopped as he struggled to think of something Steven had been good at. He finally almost mumbled a reply.

"You were a big help around the house."

"Oh, wow. What a big deal that was."

"You could have talked to me about it. When you left, your mother was frantic with worry."

"But not you, right?"

"That's not true," Max replied a little too loudly.

They both stared down at their coffee mugs as each tried to decide where to go next. Steven spoke next, shifting the conversation.

"What happened in New York?"

Max took a deep breath, struggling to face the memories he had been trying for months to bury.

"The short version? Your mother and I were having coffee at a little table in Times Square. A crazy guy began shooting. I looked for the quickest way to get your mom out of the line of fire." He paused, trying to keep control of his voice as he approached the difficult part of the narrative.

"It never occurred to me that the shooter had planted IED's around the Square. They were the real killing method. The shooting was just to start a panic and drive the crowd into his killing zones."

Max paused again before adding: "And I fell for it. Led your mother right into an explosion."

They both were silent for a moment, and then Steven spoke.

"Nobody faults you, Dad. You did the best you could."

Max shook his head.

"No, I didn't. I had better training than that. I should have known." He stopped, his voice getting weak from the effort of pushing past the lump in his throat. They both worked on their coffee before Steven suddenly looked up.

"I gotta go, dad. I can't be late."

"I understand. Thanks for calling me."

They both stood and Steven offered his hand. Max wanted desperately to hug him, but followed Steven's lead and took the offered hand.

"I'm proud of you. Captain Wouk doesn't seem like the kind of guy who would keep you aboard just to please the boss."

"No kidding," Steven said with a smile. "OK if I call you?"

"That would be great."

"Good. See you then," Steven said and hurried out the door. Max watched him go, fighting back tears and the urge to rush after him and envelop him in a bear hug. Steven passed through the door, walking out of his life for the second time.

CHAPTER 3

THE DOCKS

GALVESTON HARBOR

It was six o'clock and Max was standing on the dock as close as he could get to the *Eureka*. He had stayed in the diner after Steven left, drinking coffee and waiting for the departure time. Suddenly the horn sounded from the ship and several men on land removed ropes from cleats on the dock. The ropes immediately began to snake up toward the hull of the ship, most probably done automatically, and the ship began to slowly move away from the dock.

It was a massive ship, and as it began to slowly pass him, Max had to lean his head back so that he could see the bridge as it began to slide by. He could make out human forms behind the windows, but couldn't discern any one person. He waved anyway, knowing that Steven was up there somewhere, and jumped when the ship suddenly let out two quick blasts on its horn. He smiled and waved again. Captain Wahl was probably acknowledging his first wave.

Max stood and watched for another twenty minutes, until the ship slowly slid out of view. He took a deep breath, catching it a little as he did so. He wondered when he'd see Steven again, and worried that he hadn't done enough during their short time together to cause Steven to want to make another effort.

He turned to leave and realized that he had made no actual pan for what to do or where to go next. He had no interest in seeing Dallas, and tried to picture a road map of Texas to help decide which town to head toward next.

Putting one foot in front of the other, we began to make his way toward his bike. Two dock workers came out of a warehouse and headed toward the water. When they approached he stopped them.

"Excuse me guys. I need some advice. I'm headed from here to California, and I need a town or two in Texas to stop in along the way. Do either of you have any favorites west of here?"

The smaller of the two, which by no means made him a small man, spoke first.

"Ever been to San Anton?"

"Uh, no," replied Max.

The second man nodded his agreement.

"Charlie's right. You got stop in San Antonio. You'll love it."

"OK. Great. Thanks guys."

The two men nodded and headed off to work. Max watched them go for a moment, then turned toward his bike, already wondering how far it was to San Antonio.

CHAPTER 4

LA HACIENDA

SAN ANTONIO, TEXAS

Max was sitting at a small table in a quaint Mexican restaurant just off the River Walk in San Antonio. He had stayed on the dock in Galveston until the Eureka disappeared, then returned to his RV, packed everything, paid his bill and headed for San Antonio. He had driven on side roads instead of the interstate and finally arrived in the late afternoon. He found an RV park, selected a slip and set up shop. He had been too tired to go out again, so he made a pot of soup, had a few beers and went to bed.

The next morning he had risen early and ridden his motorcycle into town. He asked for sightseeing tips from his waitress at a diner where he had breakfast, and then spent the day visiting the Alamo and exploring the surprisingly interesting and famous River Walk. He ended up in what appeared to be a popular Mexican restaurant called La Hacienda a few blocks off the River Walk. He had always loved Mexican food, and this place had not disappointed him.

After a leisurely dinner, he lingered, enjoying several cervezas while thinking about his journey since he had lost Claire almost three months earlier. A voice brought him out of his thoughts.

"Everything OK?" his waitress asked.

"Yes," he smiled at the young girl. He guessed her to be about his daughter Charlotte's age. He glanced around and noticed that there were only a few customers remaining.

"Is it closing time?" he asked.

"Si. I'm sorry."

"Oh, no problem," he said as he glanced at his watch.

9:16 PM glowed back at him. The waitress saw him glance at his watch and explained the relatively early hour for closing.

"We open at six for breakfast, and our owner, Consuela, is our chef. She lasted longer when she was younger, but," she shrugged her shoulders and Max smiled.

"Hey, no explanations needed. I understand, believe me."

She smiled and placed a check on the table.

"I can take that whenever you're ready."

Max nodded and waited for her to leave the table before picking up the check. He examined it and was pleased that he had eaten so well for such a relatively small price. He pulled out his wallet, counted out several bills and added a very generous tip, placing it all on the table. He finished his beer just as the waitress returned.

"Please tell Consuela that I enjoyed the meal very much."

The waitress smiled.

"I will."

As she reached for the money there was a loud crash in the kitchen and the waitress jumped. It had sounded like someone had dropped a stack of dishes, and it surprised Max that the sound had so startled the waitress. He assumed the accident had happened before and should not have been such a surprise. Maybe she was new. But when he glanced at her he could see fear in her face.

Suddenly the hairs on his neck stood up, just like they had dozens of times during his time in Afghanistan, warning him of potential danger. He glanced at the door leading to the kitchen, then looked at the waitress.

"Everything OK?" he asked her.

"Si, si," she replied, a little too quickly in Max's opinion. As he stared at her there was a second crash and Max could actually see the waitress shaking. Something bad was going on in the kitchen, and Max quickly ran through his options. If the owner was having a temper tantrum, it was none of Max's business. Also if one of the employees was throwing a fit, who was Max to get involved.

But his instincts told him this was something else. He pushed his chair back and stood facing the door. The waitress sensed his intentions and grabbed his arm.

"Please, senor, it is better if you don't get involved."

Max smiled and patted her hand.

"Don't worry, dear. There's not much that could be happening on the other side of that door that I won't be able to handle."

He could see the doubt in her eyes, so he smiled even bigger and headed for the door.

CHAPTER 5

LA HACIENDA

SAN ANTONIO, TEXAS

Max stopped at the side of the door into the kitchen and gathered himself. He slowly moved his head so he could see into the kitchen. It was a rectangular room with the long sides moving away from him. There were two wide, stainless steel tables on the left and the cooking and cleaning equipment along the wall on the right. He saw three people along that wall: a young woman dressed as a waitress, a young man dressed as a cook, and a very young boy standing at the sink and dishwasher. They were all staring at the action taking place on the other side of the room.

He turned his head in that direction and saw three people, two men with their backs to him and a small woman facing him. All of the people in the room except the two men were clearly Mexican. He assumed the woman was the owner and head chef. She appeared to be middle aged and in good condition.

The man on her left was large, very overweight, and actively engaged in holding her steady while the other man spoke to her. He was shorter and very thin. As he spoke to her he periodically dropped a stack of dishes on the floor. His attempts to frighten her didn't seem to be working, so he nodded to the big man, who nodded back and began tugging her left arm behind her back. The further he pulled it, the redder her face grew, but she continued to remain silent. When the arm reached a point where Max was certain it would break soon, he pushed the door open and walked into the room.

The three people on the right side of the room looked at him and stared, but the two men and the woman ignored him. When the woman finally cried out in pain, Max had had enough.

"Hey, fat boy," he called out. "Back off."

All three of the people in the scene snapped their heads toward Max. The large man then looked at the thin man, who was obviously in charge. He looked at the large man, nodded once and tossed a glance toward Max. The large man released the woman's arm and waddled toward Max, who stood perfectly motionless. Max wasn't afraid. He had obtained plenty of knowledge in hand to hand combat during his army training, and had multiple occasions to use that training during his three tours in Afghanistan. Even though the man who was now bearing down on him significantly outweighed him, he was absolutely positive he had nowhere near Max's experience.

The man stopped less than an arm's length in front of Max.

"Who you callin' fat?" he sputtered, clearly upset.

Max calmly looked around the room and then fixed the fat man with a cold stare.

"Well, I called out hey fat boy, and you were the only one who came running, so it's pretty clear you know who I meant."

The man clenched and opened his hands at his sides as he tried to decide how to deal with Max. But Max had learned from experience to get your retaliation in first. His feet were already in the proper position, so before the fat man could decide his best course of action, Max opened a flat right hand and fired a straight arm shot directly at the man's bulbous nose. His target was the back of the man's skull, a technique he had been taught in advanced infantry training.

Most untrained people would use a closed fist and try to hit a person in the nose. First of all, there are numerous bones in a hand that can easily be broken if the fist is not properly made. And second, if the target is a person's nose, the striker tends to stop the forward movement of the strike once they make contact with the nose. Max's open hand approach, with the hand bent back, allows the strike to be made with the palm of the hand, supported by the arm. Little harm can come to the hand. And, targeting the back of the head with the nose just getting in the way keeps the strike moving forward after contact, making it much more devastating.

And it most surely was. The man's nose was shattered by the blow, as were cheek bones on both sides, and cartilage was pushed back into the brain. The large man collapsed into a heap on the floor, unconscious. Max leaned down and turned him on his side so he would not drown in his own blood, and then began moving toward the other man.

The thin man was only momentarily shocked. He quickly recovered and began reaching inside his suit jacket. Max assumed, correctly, he was moving toward a gun resting in a holster. Three quick steps put him within striking distance just as the thin man pulled the gun out of his suit coat. While it was still in front of his chest, Max used the same open hand and smashed the gun into the thin man's chest, trying to drive it into the man's back. Everyone could hear the man's rib cage cracking under the stress of the steel gun being forced into it, and the man's eyes rolled up into his head and he also collapsed on the floor.

Max looked at the woman, trying to decide if she needed any immediate medical attention, and was shocked at her reaction to his rescue.

"What are you doing?"

"Excuse me?" Max asked, confused.

"You're going to make everything worse," she almost shouted. Max blinked as she turned, picked up a cell phone lying on the floor and dialed 911.

CHAPTER 6

LA HACIENDA

SAN ANTONIO, TEXAS

The police were the first to arrive, two young men from the San Antonio Police Department. The white officer quickly checked the two injured men still on the floor while the Mexican officer separated all of the people in the room into separate spaces to be interviewed. The second officer took everyone's name and reason for being there. When he asked Max his reason, Max replied that he had heard a disturbance while eating and had entered to see what was going on.

The medics arrived, determined that both injured men needed attention and whisked them away to the local hospital. Max watched while the officers interviewed each of the other people, leaving him last. Finally the White officer approached him. He looked at his notes and then at Max.

"You are Max Walker?"

"Correct," Max replied.

"And you claim you were a customer here and heard a disturbance in here?"

"Yes."

"What kind of disturbance?"

"At first it was the sound of dishes breaking, followed by some shouting."

"So you came in?"

"Correct?"

"And then what happened?"

"The two men the medics removed were harassing the owner," Max said, pointing toward Consuela.

"And?" the cop prompted.

"And I called out to one of them, he came over and threatened me, and I put him down."

"Which one?"

"The fat one. He was the one who was holding the woman and pulling one of her arms around behind her back.

"And the other guy?"

Max shrugged.

"He pulled a gun on me, so I put him down too."

The officer stared at Max for a moment, then nodded.

"OK, Mister Walker. We're going to have to take you back to the station for further questioning."

"Why?" Max asked.

"Seems like everyone else here has a different story than yours."

"What do you mean?"

The officer glanced over at the rest of the group, now huddled together before answering.

"According to everyone else, the two men you assaulted were here discussing business with the owner, you burst in and attacked them both."

Max looked over at the group and everyone except Consuela looked away. She stared at him defiantly, daring him to argue with her.

"Interesting," Max said.

"Yeah, very," replied the officer and gave a slight twirl with his hand. "We'll need to cuff you."

"I'm under arrest?"

"Looks that way, doesn't it?"

Max stood quietly while the officer read him his rights and handcuffed him. He glanced back at Consuela once more as he was led out of the room. She continued to glare at him, and he just shook his head.

CHAPTER 7

POLICE STATION

SAN ANTONIO, TEXAS

The interrogation room felt smaller than the one in Galveston. Max realized this was his second visit to a police interrogation room in one week. He hoped this wasn't the beginning of a trend. He had been there for over an hour, and it was getting close to midnight. He wondered when he'd get some sleep.

The lock on the lone door clicked and the door opened. Nothing happened for several moments, and then a tall, well-dressed man entered and closed the door behind him. He turned and looked at Max. He was a good-looking man. His dark hair was meticulously combed and his pencil thin mustache was the same dark color. His deep tan held it all together for a very good look.

He finished looking at Max, sat down and placed a folder on the desk.

"So, Mister Walker, I understand you were read your rights at the scene?"

"Correct," Max replied. "And you are?"

"Ah, sorry. Detective Wolf. Dave Wolf."

Max just nodded and Wolf continued.

"Do you want to speak to an attorney before we go on?"

Max shook his head.

"Let's talk first. I'll let you know if I need an attorney."

"Excellent. Let's begin with a little background," Wolf said and opened the folder. He peered at the top page.

"You've had quite an exciting time the last few months." He paused and looked at Max, who just stared back and waited.

"Right. Seems to have started with some sort of adventure in Key West, which turned into a kidnapping in Galveston, which the police foiled." He paused again and looked up, but Max remained silent.

"The whole thing after the attempted kidnap moved remarkably quickly. Probably had something to do with the fact that you were represented by Marcia Fullbright, who happens to be the best known lawyer in the South."

He stopped again and nodded several times before continuing.

"She was also involved in getting charges dropped against your son. Some pretty serious charges."

He looked up and stared at Max as he continued.

"You going to call her again when you decide to involve a lawyer?"

"I'm hoping we can clear this up without a lawyer," Max replied. Wolf shook his head.

"Not much chance of that. The guys in the hospital are pressing charges. Aggravated assault. Pretty serious. Lots of witnesses who all saw the same thing."

"What do they say happened?"

"They were doing regular business in the kitchen. All of a sudden you burst in and attacked the two men, putting both in the hospital."

Max stared at Wolf, then shook his head.

"I was having dinner when I heard a ruckus in the kitchen."

"What kind of ruckus?" Wolf asked.

"Dishes breaking. Lots of them."

"Happens all the time in kitchens," Wolf tossed in.

"Not half dozen times."

Wolf shrugged.

"And then?"

"I went to the door and looked in. The cook and a waitress and a bus boy were all on the right, watching these two goons strong arming the owner."

Wolf shook his head.

"Strong arming?"

"Yeah. The fat guy was holding her one arm and bending the other one behind her back while the skinny guy was in her face saying something and dropping dishes on the floor."

"So you just charged in and put them both in the hospital."

Max stared at Wolf.

"They were hurting her. So I went in and called to the fat guy. He came over to me and prepared to take a swing at me, so I hit him first."

"And the skinny guy?" Wolf prompted.

"He pulled a gun on me, so I disarmed him."

Wolf shook his head.

"We didn't find a gun anywhere."

Max stopped and sat back. He wasn't sure what was going on, but it was clear he wasn't leaving the station tonight.

"I think it's time for me to see a lawyer."

Wolf nodded.

"Want me to call Miss Fullbright for you?" he asked in a snide voice. Max pictured Marcia getting up from the table and walking out at their lunch. He shook his head.

"Who then?" asked Wolf.

"I'll start with the public defender and go from there."

"OK," Wolf said and stood. "I'll have someone come by and take you to a cell. It's too late to get anyone here tonight."

Max nodded and watched Wolf leave the room. He heard the lock click and closed his eyes.

"Well", he said out loud. "Chalk up another life experience." He closed his eyes and sat back to wait to be taken to his cell.

CHAPTER 8

POLICE STATION

SAN ANTONIO, TEXAS

Breakfast had been too early in the morning and inedible, so Max wasn't in the best of moods when the outer door to the cell block opened and a guard sauntered in, followed by a middle aged man in a badly fitting suit carrying a battered briefcase. Max sighed. This must be his court appointed lawyer. As the two approached Max stood up and tried to look decent.

The guard stopped at the door to his cell and fumbled for a specific key from a ring of keys in his hand. He spoke to Max as he found the key and unlocked the door.

"Mister Walker, this is your lawyer. He'll fill you in on what happens next, OK?"

Max nodded.

"Great," he said as he turned around and walked the three steps back to his bunk. The lawyer entered and dragged a chair in behind him. He sat down as the guard locked the door and walked out of the room. The lawyer put his briefcase on his lap, opened it and pulled out a file. Max watched him, not really paying attention to the man himself. All Max saw was a thin black man who didn't really look comfortable in his suit, or in the cell for that matter. Finally the lawyer spoke.

"I was hoping for a little more excitement from you when you saw me."

Max squinted at the man's face for the first time. Something stirred at the back of his brain and he leaned forward to study the man better. After a few seconds the man smiled and recognition popped onto Max's face.

"Sing? Singleton Harris? Is that you?"

The man's smile broadened.

"In the flesh."

Max jumped up off the bed and grabbed the man's hand.

"What the hell are you doing here?" Max asked as memories flooded over him. Harris had been in his squad the entire time he had been in Afghanistan. He had been a poor kid from East St. Louis who talked fast and could run even faster. He'd been a good soldier and they had gone through a lot together.

"No, Sarge, that's my line to you," Harris said still smiling.

Max nodded.

"Long story. But first, how the hell did you get here? The last time I saw you, you were thinking about signing on for one more tour in 'stan'."

Harris leaned back and his eyes seemed to drift away.

"Long time ago, Sarge. You went home and I was thinking about signing up again. About three days after you left our Humvee was hit by an IED. I took some shit in my right leg and got sent home. Army decided they would give me a job stateside and send me to school if stayed in." He stopped and shrugged. "So I did. Took a while but first got my high school diploma, then a college degree, and then I went to law school."

"And now you're a lawyer?"

"Yup. Working as a public defender, trying to.." he stopped suddenly and glanced away. Max knew why and finished the sentence for him.

"Trying to learn the ropes before you go into private practice."

Harris looked back at Max with a sheepish grin.

"Been at it over a year now. I've learned a lot."

"Terrific," Max said and lay back on his bed. This was going to be harder than he thought.

CHAPTER

POLICE STATION

SAN ANTONIO, TEXAS

Max spent an hour bringing Harris up to speed on what had been going on in his life from the attack in New York City up to the scene in the restaurant kitchen. Harris took notes and sat quietly for a moment when Max finished before responding.

"Why do you suppose they all lied?"

"I have no idea."

Harris nodded, puffed out his cheeks and cleared his throat, trying to prepare to ask what he expected to be a difficult question.

"Sounds like we're goin' to need some help. Can you, uh, afford to pay for a private investigator?"

"What do you have in mind?"

"I've got a friend that does work for me here in town from time to time, but he's pretty expensive, least by my standards."

"What's pretty expensive?"

"Could be five hundred a day," Harris said quietly, already preparing for Max to object.

"OK, if you think we need him."

"Really?" Harris said, perking up. "Awesome. You'll like this guy and he'll get to the bottom of what's going on, for sure."

"What's his name?"

"Elliott."

"Elliott what?"

"No, that's his last name."

"What's his first name?"

Harris hesitated.

"Not sure really. He goes by Elliott."

Max just nodded. Suddenly the outer door opened and the officer who had brought Harris in stuck his head through the opening.

"Your times up, councilor."

"Got it," Harris shouted back. The door closed and then reopened and the guard walked in. Harris stood.

"I'll be back in the morning. We got a hearing at ten. I'll try to get a decent bail figure. You got some extra money to pay bail, or anyone who will put up the money for you?"

Max nodded. He couldn't wait to get out of jail.

"Yeah, I can make bail. Just get it done."

Harris nodded, they shook hands and suddenly Max was alone again.

CHAPTER 10

COURT HOUSE

SAN ANTONIO, TEXAS

Judge Thaddeus Conway was glaring at Harris.

"Mister Harris, we haven't even begun the proceedings this morning and you have already insulted me and my court."

Harris looked up from the papers he had been organizing.

"How so, Judge?"

Conway nodded toward Max.

"Is this how you were taught in law school to prepare your client for his first court appearance?"

Harris glanced at Max, who was wearing the same clothes he had been wearing when he was arrested almost three days earlier. He was also unshaven and his hair was wild.

"Your honor, my client's appearance was going to be in my opening statement. I am appalled by how he has been treated. He's not been allowed to change clothes, even into an orange jumpsuit. He's not been allowed a comb, a tooth brush, a shower, nothing."

Conway turned his ire toward the prosecutor. He didn't need to say a word. Dalton Webber jumped to his feet.

"Your honor. I'm just as shocked as you are to see the condition of the prisoner. I suggest we adjourn and give him time to get cleaned up."

Harris shook his head, realizing he now had an advantage.

"Your honor, if you can possibly see a way to just continue, I think it would be better for my client. He's already suffered the embarrassment of his appearance. He'll never be able to get himself cleaned up, at least not to his normal standards, at the jail."

Conway stared at Harris, then nodded.

"All right. Let's move forward."

The prosecutor read the charges, the judge asked how Max pled, and Harris replied the expected 'Not guilty', and the judge bound the case over for trial, and set a date several months in the future. Harris took a deep breath.

"Your honor. I request that my client be released on bail."

Webber instantly replied.

"Your honor, the accused is a flight risk. He's only been in town one day. He's from Ohio." He said the last word with such disgust that a casual observer might think the place was somewhere in Russia. Conway looked back at Harris for a rebuttal. He spread his hands wide as he replied.

"Your honor, my client has recently suffered the tragedy of the loss of his wife in the terrorist attack in New York City. He's on his way to California to see his only daughter who's attending Stanford University."

"He could still be a flight risk," Conway replied.

"He's also a veteran, your honor. In fact, I served two tours with the defendant in Afghanistan. He was my sergeant. If he says he'll stay here, he'll stay here."

The judge looked back and forth between the two lawyers, raised his gavel and gave his decision.

"Bail is set at five hundred thousand" he said and banged the gavel down. Harris started to object but Conway was already standing up.

"All rise," the court bailiff called out. Everyone stood and Conway disappeared through the door behind the bench.

Harris turned a sad face to Max.

"Sorry man."

"Why?" Max asked.

"Where you goin' to get that kind of money?"

"I only need ten percent of that for a bail bondsman, right?"

"Well, yeah, but still. Fifty grand?"

"Just get me to my RV."

"Seriously?"

Max nodded.

"Have I ever lied to you Sing?"

Harris smiled.

"Not once."

"All right," he said as the officer stepped up to escort Max back to the jail.

"I'll meet you at the jail. I can't get you out without the money, but if you can tell me where it is, we'll be good."

Max studied Harris's face. He thought of the huge amount of cash hidden in the RV and the risk of telling anyone, even his lawyer, where it was. But then he thought of all the times he had trusted this same man with his life in Afghanistan and nodded.

"See you there," he said and was led out by the policeman.

Harris watched them go and smiled again. He might just get paid for this job after all.

CHAPTER 11

STARBUCKS

SAN ANTONIO, TEXAS

It was two days later and Max was sitting in a Starbucks with Singleton Harris and Elliott, a very large man with medium long, dark black hair, and strong brown eyes. Max had given Harris the information he needed to get into *Spirit*, Max's RV and find one of the caches of cash Max had stashed away. Harris had used the money to post bail for Max and pay a retainer fee to Elliott, the PI Harris used when his clients could afford it. Max had been released the day before and had spent most of the remainder of the day getting rid of the smell of the jail that had lingered on his body.

"So," Harris was saying, "Elliott has been busy the last few days."

Max turned to look at Elliott and started slightly. Elliott's brown eyes were fixed so hard on Max's face that he could almost feel heat from them. He decided to wait for Elliott to speak. After a few seconds that seemed like an eternity, he opened his mouth and a strong, deep base voice forced itself into the space between them.

"Seems like you inserted yourself into the middle of a turf war."

"What do you mean?" Max asked.

"The two men you messed up were in the process of explaining to the restaurant owner that she would no

40

longer be paying protection money to the Mexican mafia, but would be paying the regular mafia instead."

Max glanced at Harris, who nodded.

"Are you serious?"

"As a heart attack."

"That stuff still goes on?"

"Every day."

"But what about the police?" Max asked. Elliott rolled his eyes.

"They either won't or can't stop it. Many possible reasons why."

Max stared at Elliott for some time before turning to Harris.

"So what do we do about it?"

"About what?" Harris asked.

"Have you been listening?" Max snapped back, then closed his eyes. "Sorry."

"No need to be," Harris replied. "What do you think you can do?"

"Well, we can't just let them get away with this?"

Elliott broke in.

"Short term, you could move into her kitchen and keep them away, but eventually you'll move on. Then what?"

"How do we stop them then?" Max asked.

"Exactly," replied Elliott.

Max shook his head. He stood up, glanced around the room and then spoke in a hard voice.

"Not acceptable."

He turned and walked out. Harris and Elliott watched him go, then Elliott turned to Harris.

"What'll he do now?"

"I don't know yet, but believe me. Whatever it is, you'll hear about it."

Elliott nodded.

"He's getting in over his head."

"Don't sell Sarge short."

"He's one guy."

"At the moment. He's also very resourceful".

Elliott stared at Harris for a moment, then they both finished their coffee and left.

CHAPTER 12

LA HACIENDA

SAN ANTONIO, TEXAS

Max had finished his meal and was waiting patiently for the waitress to return. He had paid the bill and asked to see the owner, Consuela. He wanted to talk to her about what he could do to help. After a few minutes the waitress returned with a serious face. She shook her head at Max.

"I'm terribly sorry sir, but she won't see you."

"Why not?"

"She claims that you will only cause more trouble for her."

"But I'm trying to help her get out of this trouble."

"She doesn't think that is possible, especially by only one man."

Max nodded his head.

"OK. Do you happen to know when the people she is so afraid of will be back?"

The waitress glanced at the door to the kitchen with a worried look. She turned back and studied Max for a moment before responding.

"You didn't hear this from me, OK?"

"Of course."

"They said they'd be back tomorrow after closing."

"OK."

"The problem is, the other guys usually come back on Thursdays too."

"About the same time?"

She shook her head.

"No. They usually come about an hour later, just when everything is ready to close."

"Huh," Max said out loud. A true turf war going on, and Consuela was caught in the middle.

"Please be careful, sir."

Max nodded his agreement.

"I always am. Don't worry. No one will get hurt."

The waitress nodded and then moved to another table at the call from a customer.

"No one that doesn't deserve it, that is," Max said quietly to himself and stood up. He looked around once again and left the restaurant.

CHAPTER 13

LA HACIENDA

SAN ANTONIO, TEXAS

Max was standing in the shadows in an alley about fifty yards from the back entrance to La Hacienda. He was surprised at how cool it was getting now that the sun was down. He checked his watch.

9:10 PM

He shrugged further down into his clothes. Recon was not his favorite past time. It was boring, tiring, rarely provided the information needed to make a solid decision, and sometimes it was dangerous. A black car turned into the alley at the other end and moved slowly toward him, stopping forty yards away outside the rear entrance to La Hacienda. He pushed himself closer to the wall, hiding in the shadows.

The two back doors opened and one man got out from each side. Max could still see the shapes of two more heads in the car. The two that got out walked to the door, looked up and down the alley, then opened the door and went in. Max considered what he had seen. The two men were both short, stocky and moved with the visible energy of youth. He couldn't tell much about the two left in the car, a late model Toyota from what he could tell.

Less than five minutes later the door opened and the two men walked out, paused to look in both directions, and then returned to the car. It slowly backed out of the alley and turned right, disappearing from view. Max glanced at his watch.

9:20.

It hadn't taken them long. Max wondered if the mafia men would be as prompt and efficient as the Mexicans. At 9:30 another car, also black, pulled into the alley and stopped at the same place as the previous one. This was a new Mercedes, also with four men in it. Max watched a rerun of what had happened earlier, except these two men were much taller, lean and not as concerned about what else might be in the alley. By 9:30 the second group had departed.

Max waited another ten minutes to be certain there was no one else watching the alley. He stepped out of the shadows and began walking toward the street. He stopped at the door to *La Hacienda* and tugged on it. It was locked. He nodded and walked to the end of the alley, glanced both ways, turned right and continued walking. After about fifty yards a car pulled alongside and slowed to match his pace. He glanced over at the car, another black car.

The passenger window slid down and he heard a man's voice.

"Get in the car, Max."

Max stopped. He recognized the voice. Bending down, he looked into the car and saw Elliott staring back at him. He stood up, opened the door and slid in. The car moved away from the curb as Elliott glanced at Max.

"Find out what you wanted to know? You saw both groups?"

"You were watching me?"

Elliott shrugged.

"Just protecting my investment. You owe me for two days work."

Max glanced over and saw the smile on Elliott's face.

"Was I that easy to follow?"

Elliott shrugged.

"I figured you'd be here watching."

Max nodded.

"Take me to the RV Park. We'll have a beer or two and talk."

"Sounds liked a plan," Elliott said and turned at the next corner, heading out of town.

CHAPTER 15

STARLIGHT RV PARK

SAN ANTONIO, TEXAS

Elliott and Max were seated at the small dining table in *Spirit*, Max's RV. Elliott was asking the questions.

"What exactly do you expect to accomplish here long term?"

Max took a short pull on his beer before answering.

"I don't expect to stop these guys from extorting the restaurants in town. The cops should be doing that. All I want to do is get them to stop bothering La Hacienda."

"You have a thing for the owner?"

Max shook his head.

"Don't even know her. And the only time we talked she pretty much told me to get lost. Told me I was making things worse for her."

"So, why do you care?"

Max thought about it. He'd been asking himself the same thing.

"I suppose it goes back to my experiences in Afghanistan. We'd come into some tiny village that the bad guys had just been in, and it was a mess. The buildings were all trashed, and the people were even worse. And they were all scared. "

He paused and took another drink, then shrugged.

"I guess I don't like it much when somebody strong arms a weaker person and makes them fear everything. It's not right."

"An avenging angel?"

"Hardly," Max snorted. "Just somebody who wants the weak to have a little peace, that's all."

Elliott nodded.

"Understood. But it still comes down to what are you planning to do when you leave town?"

Max took a deep breath and exhaled.

"We had the same problem in 'Stan'. We'd run the bad guys out and as soon as we left they'd move back in."

"So, what'd you do about it?"

"We set up a deterrent system."

"Like what?"

"We'd find the base of the leader of the local group of bad guys, and every time they attacked another village, we'd call in an air strike and pound the crap out of them. Made it worse than what it was worth to attack the villages."

"So, you used drones?"

"Yeah, sometimes."

"Too bad we don't have any now."

Max nodded and then looked up sharply at Elliott.

"What?" Elliott said.

"You know, drones might just be the thing we need here." He smiled and Elliott gave him an odd look.

"I'll make some calls," Max said and took another pull on his beer, a soft smile spreading over his face.

CHAPTER 16

STARLIGHT RV PARK

SAN ANTONIO, TEXAS

Elliott was gone and Max picked up his phone, scrolled through his list and punched a call. It was answered after two rings.

"Yeah?"

"Hey, Zeke, this is Max Walker."

"Already knew that. That's what caller ID is for."

"I need a favor," Max continued.

"Already figured that. If you wanted to chat you'd a called your daughter."

Max took deep breath. He was beginning to understand why his friend Drew McGee didn't like to call this man.

"OK, I'll get right to it."

"Wonderful," Zeke broke in.

"I need to do some covert surveillance, from the air."

"You need a drone."

"Right. It has to be a good one, silent, can carry a video camera."

"Kind a hard to do surveillance without a camera."

Max sighed again and decided to let Zeke ask the questions.

"Terrain?" Zeke asked.

"What?"

"City or country?"

"Oh, small city. San Antonio."

"Surveilling bad guys?"

"Correct. I want to follow a few collectors back to their base so I can ID their leader."

"Timing?"

"ASAP."

Max could hear computer keys being tapped as Zeke continued.

"A PROTEC 2100 is what you need. It'll deliver live feed back to your cellphone and keep a copy on its hard drive. And I can program a few extra goodies into it if you can give me one day."

Max started to ask a question but Zeke continued.

"A little pricey, probably around a grand to get it there by the day after tomorrow by noon. Use your pay pal account that Drew set up?"

"Yes."

"Done. Anything else?"

"No. Guess that's all," Max said and the line disconnected. Max held the phone away from his ear and stared at it.

"Rude SOB" he said out loud and tapped his phone to close his end of the call. He put it out of his mind and pulled out a pen and paper and began to make notes. He had a day and a half to figure out a plan.

CHAPTER 17

SECLUDED AREA

NEAR COMFORT, TEXAS

Max was sitting on a boulder looking out over a large area of scrub bush, dry land and small hills, nothing in sight for as far as he could see. He turned to Elliott and nodded.

"This is perfect."

"Good," Elliott nodded and continued. "I like it because it's not too far north of the city but still not much going on around here, nobody to see you practicing with your new toy."

Max nodded his agreement and took another look at the extensive directions that came along with his new toy. The set included by the manufacturer were fairly clear, but the ones added by Zeke were a little hard to follow, mostly because he wrote in computer jargon instead of plain English.

"Wish I knew what the hell he is talking about," Max said and tossed the pages toward Elliott. "Can you figure it out?"

Elliott grabbed the papers.

"Why don't you just call him and ask him to explain it?"

"Huh," Max grumbled. "You don't know this guy."

"A prima donna?"

"You have no idea."

Elliott nodded and tugged out his phone. He hit a speed dial number and waited.

"Lo" came a response.

"Jane, I need you to translate for me".

"Not now, dad."

"Yes, now. It's important. I'm here with a client, the one I told you about who's trying to help the owner of La Hacienda?"

"Oh, OK. Can we make it quick?"

Elliott proceeded to read Zeke's printed directions and took notes in the margins as his daughter rattled off explanations. When they were finished he nodded.

"Thanks, hun."

"Later, dad."

Elliott put the phone away and looked at Max.

"Done."

"How does she know what Zeke is talking about?"

"She's a Georgia Tech grad. Can write code if you want her to. Knows everything about computers and how to talk to them or about them."

Max nodded and Elliott turned toward the drone.

"OK. Let's get this thing set up, shall we?"

They put their heads together and began to work.

CHAPTER 18

SECLUDED AREA

NEAR COMFORT, TEXAS

Two hours later Max felt comfortable that everything was ready for a trial run. He turned to Elliott

"Ready?"

"Seems like it."

Max nodded and opened one of the two cardboard boxes sitting next to them. He pulled out a small container and opened it. After peering inside, he gently took out a small clear capsule.

"What's that?" Elliott asked.

"Some enzyme or something that Zeke had sent to me. I'm supposed to somehow get one of these in contact with whoever I want the drone to follow. On their skin. The capsule dissolves almost instantly and the liquid permeates the skin. Nothing visible, but it's there and the drone can track it."

"How long does it last?"

"Supposedly about two weeks."

"Wow."

Max nodded and opened the second box. With his empty hand he reached in and pulled out a small rabbit.

"Where'd you get that?" Elliott asked.

"A pet store in town. I was assured that he'll run away if we free him."

He held the rabbit in one hand and pushed the capsule onto its right shoulder. He looked at Elliott.

"Well, here goes nothing."

He put the rabbit down one the ground. It looked around for a moment or two and then took off toward a nearby clump of brush. Max peered at the control switch for the drone, tapped *self-control* and the drone sprang to life. It easily lifted off the ground, hovered over them at about ten feet for a few seconds, and then lifted to about fifty feet and began to slowly move away from them. Max tapped his phone and the screen came to life with a clear picture of the land around them, as seen from above.

"It's following the rabbit," he said to Elliott and turned the face for him to see.

"And it's recording everything?"

"Yeah. We can access it anytime we want."

"So you have to somehow get one of these gels onto the skin of one of the bad guys and the drone will follow him wherever he goes?"

"Right."

"And we're doing this to try to find out where the headquarters is for these guys and who's in charge?"

"Yes."

"But we're not going to try to get rid of all of these guys ourselves, right?"

"Right. They have to be into a lot of bad stuff. I'm assuming drugs are involved. If the locals won't do anything, we will get the DEA involved. Harris says he knows someone there. He went to law school with a guy who he can talk to."

Elliott nodded and went back to his original line of questioning.

"What if the guy doesn't go to the headquarters? What if he just goes to a middle man?"

"The drone's computer tags everyone he comes in contact with and follows them too. It runs a program to determine if the new person is part of the system or not. It drops them if it thinks they are superfluous."

"What if it takes a day or two to get to the right guy?"

"It generates its own power, so it can hang up there for as long as it takes."

"Seems like it would have to go pretty high to cover all the ground it might need to."

"Right."

"And it won't lose the signal if it goes really high?"

"I'm told that's not a problem."

Elliott looked up at the sky.

"You know, if you can do this, the government certainly can."

"For sure."

"So, who are they watching right now?"

"Not us, I hope," Max said with a smile.

Elliott just nodded and they watched the drone as it slowly climbed and followed the rabbit.

"Seen enough?" Max asked. Elliott nodded and Max picked up the control pad and brought the drone back to their position. As he packed everything up, he thought about the mission ahead.

"Just like the old days in Afghanistan," he said out loud.

"Except hopefully no one is shooting back," Elliott said in a serious tone.

"Hopefully," Max replied and continued to pack up for the trip back to town.

CHAPTER 19

HARRIS'S APARTMENT

SAN ANTONIO, TEXAS

The three men sat around the small table in the even smaller kitchen of Singleton Harris's apartment. They were trying to work out the details of placing the tracing gel on the bag men representing the two groups of thugs that were fleecing Consuela dry.

"I still think we should use two different people for this job, one for the Mexicans and one for the Mafia," Harris said.

"But why?" replied Max. "I can do both of them. It'll be different men on different nights. Nobody will be able to make me from the first one."

"That may be true," Elliott interjected. "But it's still you taking all of the risk. I think you should do one and let me do the other."

They had been arguing the point for over ten minutes when the door to the bedroom opened and a young woman walked into the kitchen.

"Michele!" Harris almost gasped. "What are you doing here?"

The woman smiled sheepishly at Harris.

"I am so sorry, Mister Harris. I fell asleep waiting for the sheets to finish in the dryer, and I just now finished."

Both men looked at Harris for an explanation.

60

"Michele is my cleaning woman. She comes twice a week." He paused and shot her a nervous look, wondering if she had heard their conversation.

"I'm finished now," she said and stood looking at him. He realized it was Friday and he regularly paid her at the end of each week. He jumped up.

"I'll get your envelope," he said and disappeared into his tiny office. Max looked at Michele, also wondering if she had been listening. She smiled back at him.

"You must be Max."

"Yes, I am," Max answered cautiously.

"Mister Harris has told me a little about you. You were his sergeant in the army."

"Uh, yes, I was."

"And now you must be a writer or something."

"Why do you say that?"

Michele shrugged.

"I heard a little of your conversation. You were trying to work out a tricky scene. Something about sneaking a secret gel onto some bad men so you could follow them. Sounded like a spy thriller."

Elliott jumped in immediately.

"Exactly, Michele." He glanced at Harris as he returned. "We were helping Max work out a scene for his new book. But, you can't tell anyone. Max is pretty famous and if another writer heard about the scene they might steal it for their own book."

Michele tapped her lips.

"My lips are sealed."

Harris handed her an envelope.

"Here you go, Michele. Thank you."

"Thank you, Mister Harris."

She turned to leave and then stopped.

"I assumed it is a spy thriller, written mostly for men, right?"

"Why do you say that?" Max asked.

"Well, it sounded like a real guy thing you were talking about."

"What do you mean?" Elliott asked.

"Well, you know. Which one should take the big risk, placing the gel on the bad guys, and all?"

Elliott just shook his head as if he didn't understand.

Michele continued.

"Because the whole thing isn't logical."

"Why not?" Max asked.

"Well, the character needs to get the gel on the bag men so the computer can follow them back to their meeting place, where it will then pick up everybody they come in contact with and follow them until you get the top bad guys, right?"

They all looked at each other in dismay. Harris spoke first.

“You were listening for some time, Michele.”

She glanced down and then looked him in the eye.

“Sorry.”

Max jumped in.

“Why is that such a guy thing?”

“Because, you don’t really have to take any risk at all.”

“Whys that?”

She shrugged.

“Just put the gel on the person who they are getting the money from. When they come in contact with her, the computer tags them and that’s all you need, right?”

Max looked at Elliott, who looked like he wished he could slap his forehead.

“Well, yeah, I guess that would work.”

“But what if she won’t do it?” Harris asked.

Michele shrugged.

“You could put it on the waitress. When she goes into the kitchen, the computer would pick up everybody and you’d eventually get the bad guys.”

Max just nodded and she continued before he could say anything.

“In fact, you could just wear the gel yourself and go have dinner there on the right night. The waitress comes over, she gets tagged, and you’re set.”

She smiled and Max nodded. He glanced at Harris.

"So, Michele, are you done for the day?"

"Yes."

"Do you have a few more minutes to chat with us?"

"I do."

"Have a seat," Max said and pulled out the remaining chair. "Would you like something to drink?"

"Please."

Max glanced at Harris, who shrugged at stood. He walked to the refrigerator.

"Iced tea, or water?"

Michele hesitated, the replied.

"The Hennessy is in the cabinet in the living room, second shelf."

Harris turned at stared at her. Max broke into a grin.

"That's a great idea, Michele." He looked at Harris.

"Hennessy for everyone, Harris."

Harris slumped and walked into the living room as Michele took a seat at the table.

CHAPTER 20

LA HACIENDA

SAN ANTONIO, TEXAS

Elliott had been elected to deliver the tracing gel to the restaurant. He sat at a table by himself near the front door. The waitress had just taken his order and headed to the kitchen. He glanced around the room to make sure no one was watching him. Satisfied, he slipped the gel packet out of his pocket, broke open the seal and placed the packet on the back of his right hand. He watched as the slightly blue semi-liquid flared slightly and then totally disappeared.

The waitress returned about ten minutes later with his order. He kept his right hand on the table as she placed his food. He had listened intently when Zeke had briefed the three of them the night before on the phone and he was confident he had prepared everything correctly. He smiled and thanked the waitress and watched as she went to take another order.

'Extra subjects' he thought to himself. The computer would begin following all of the customers the waitress came in contact with in addition to their target subjects. Elliott sat tensely until the waitress returned to the kitchen. He took a deep breath and tried to relax. He had executed his part of the plan. Now it was up to technology to begin filling out the profile of what the Mexican gang was up to. Tomorrow Harris would dine here and place the second gel tracker in order to track the Mafia gang. Zeke had asked that the two be kept separate, and they had all agreed.

Elliott shook his head as he marveled at the space age technology he had just set into place. He absently took a bite of his Chimichanga and his attention snapped to the present.

"This is awesome" he mumbled to himself and settled in to enjoy his dinner and the Dos Equis beer.

CHAPTER 21

HARRIS'S KITCHEN

SAN ANTONIO, TEXAS

Harris finished making coffee, filled three cups and sat down at the table. Elliott looked around the space and smiled.

"Michele not here today?"

Harris gave him a 'don't even go there' look but Max picked up on the subject.

"Well, if she's not coming, where'll we get any good ideas on what to do next?"

"You guys going to bust my chops on this forever?" Harris retorted. Max shook his head.

"OK, let's get to it."

He picked up a small carry bag from the floor and pulled out a laptop. He put it on the table and opened it, then fiddled with the keys. A map of the San Antonio area appeared on the screen and he turned the computer around so both Elliott and Harris could see it. Harris squinted at the screen and then sat back.

"Damn. There's got to be five hundred little red and blue dots on there."

"Right. The red dots are the Mexican contacts and the Blue ones are the Mafia."

Elliott had been studying the screen and now spoke.

"Interesting."

"What?"

"The two colors don't cross much except along the River Walk."

"Where all the restaurants are," Max added.

"This has only been up for what, two days?" Harris asked.

"Right," replied Max.

"So how we goin' to read this thing after a week or so? It'll be solid red and blue. Won't even be able to read the map."

Max nodded, reached forward and tapped few keys. The screen went blank for a moment and then reappeared with only a few red dots on it.

"This shows only the first two guys Elliott tagged."

"Better," Harris said and then pointed to the left section of the screen where a column of writing appeared.

"What's that?"

Max looked and sat back again.

"Actually, this is amazing. The computer follows each dot, and by extrapolating from where they go and how long they stay there, it can figure out where the person lives. It then checks files and figures out the name of the person the dot represents."

"You're kidding me," Elliott jumped in.

"No," Max said, shaking his head. "I talked to the programmer last night, a girl named Zannie. She's a friend of Drew and Zeke. This whole thing is a project she's working on for her doctorate in mathematics."

"This is awesome!" was all Harris could say, but Elliott became very excited.

"So, we'll be able to give the DEA people not only where these guys have been, but what their names are?"

"Uh huh," Max said, smiling. "And that's not all, Zannie said the program will predict what they are doing at each site. So, if any of them are into trafficking drugs, the program will confirm that and also tell where and when they do it."

Harris just shook his head.

"Pretty scary stuff."

"Yeah," Max confirmed. "You wouldn't believe the stuff I've learned since I picked up Drew hitchhiking a few weeks ago."

"So what do we do next?"

"Zannie suggested that we do a little on site recon before we approach the Feds. Just to confirm the computer's conclusions."

"You mean, like, go to the place where they're allegedly selling drugs and check it out?"

"Yep."

"When are we doing that?" Harris asked.

"You're not doing it at all. Too risky to your profession if you are seen. Elliott and I will handle the recon." He glanced at Elliott.

"We'll split it up. You want the Mexicans or the Mafia?"

Elliott smiled.

"I'll do the Mexicans."

"OK. Just curious, why'd you pick them?"

"Lost a brother awhile back. He got caught in a crossfire that the police claimed was a turf war." He glanced at the screen and continued. "Pretty close to where some of these guys are going."

"Don't let this get personal," Max warned.

"Isn't that what you've been doing since the beginning of all this?" Elliott retorted.

Max stared at him for a moment before answering.

"OK, you take the Mexicans. I'll follow the Mafia guys. And we need photos if we can get them."

"Why?" Harris asked.

"Zannie asked me to get some. She said by tomorrow the computer will have found photos and will be posting them on the screen next to each guys bio. She'd like to see a few to see how good her software is."

Harris shook his head.

"Geeks."

"I know, right?" Max said and took a sip of his coffee.

"Good stuff Harris," he said and raised the mug in salute.

"Better'n anything we ever got in the Army."

"Setting a pretty low standard there, aren't you?"

"Only in the area of coffee, my man."

Max nodded and they went back to work planning the evenings activities.

CHAPTER 22

72

TENAMENT HOUSING

SAN ANTONIO, TEXAS

Max was using a long lens on his Leica camera to get shots of both buyers and sellers doing a brisk business a block away. Most of the traffic was obviously from the affluent suburbs judging by the slow parade of Mercedes, Lexus and BMW's. The customer would pull up to a corner where a very young white boy would step up to the driver side window. Money was passed out to the boy and he would listen, then nod and run to a nearby house and disappear inside.

The customer would drive down the block to a point and wait. Another white boy, a little older but still under the age of eighteen, would run out and hand a package through the window to the customer. The window would go up and the car would drive away. As he watched Max assumed that Elliott was having the same scene play out at his stake out, except the boys were probably Mexicans.

He wasn't getting very many good shots of the drivers of the cars, but he was getting very clear records of the make of the car and the license plate. After recording about an hour of this, he put the rental car into gear and drove to the second spot frequented by the red dots. This turned out to be the same kind of transactions, except the neighborhood was even lower class, the customers were on foot and the runners were all black.

Here Max was getting great shots of the faces of the customers. While shooting the sixth customer, he pulled the camera away from his face and peered at the scene, then put the camera back to his eye for a better look. He took a deep breath as he realized he recognized the buyer. It was the dishwasher from La Hacienda. He shook his head and made a mental note to mention it to Sing and Elliott during their nightly meeting. He spent another half hour recording faces before tiring and calling it a day.

CHAPTER 23

HARRIS APARTMENT

SAN ANTONIO, TEXAS

The Pizza delivery man and the FedEx driver arrived at the same time. Harris answered the door, paid the pizza boy, who was expected, and signed for the FedEx package that was not. He carried the large package from FedEx with the pizzas sitting on top and put everything on the kitchen table where Max and Elliott were waiting.

"What's this?" Elliott asked.

"Peperoni and double cheese on one and plain on the other," Harris replied.

"No, I mean the big box."

"No idea. It's addressed to Max, care of me," he said, looking at Max expectantly.

"Don't ask me," Max replied.

"Just open the damn thing," Elliott said and Max followed the order. Inside was a second drone, exactly like the one already flying over San Antonio. Max picked out the enclosed letter and opened it. He read it quickly and gave a running commentary to the other two.

"It's from Zannie. She wants it in the air ASAP. We're supposed to call her when it's up. She plans to move all of the red targets to it, and leave all of the blue targets on the other drone. Says it will make it easier because each one will have less geography to cover."

"Makes sense to me," Elliott said, nodding his approval. Max smiled and continued.

"The Cornell science lab picked up the tab for this one. They got a grant from the government. They seem to see the potential of the process and will be very interested in the data when she's ready to present."

"When will that be?" Harris asked.

"Doesn't say," Max replied.

"Well, I hope she's in a hurry, because this is going to be our best defense to get you off the assault charges."

Max nodded. He could already see the likelihood of trading this information for his release from the charges. Harris began setting out plates and utensils for the pizza. Suddenly the door flew open and Michele rushed in.

"Sorry I'm late. Have you started yet?"

Elliott and Max looked at Harris, who shrugged.

"She'll stay quiet if we keep her in the loop. Otherwise..."

Max took a deep breath and let it out slowly. He looked at Michele and cocked his head.

"I just have one question."

Everyone held their breath, Michele with a pained look on her face.

"Yes?" she said quietly.

"Do you like pepperoni or plain?"

CHAPTER 24

HARRIS APARTMENT

SAN ANTONIO, TEXAS

"So, what are we talking about today?" Michele asked as she pulled up a chair and sat down. Before anyone could answer she continued. "Wow! Is this the drone that's been flying around?"

Max shook his head.

"It's a new one. We need two so we can split the coverage. Elliott and I are going to drive out and launch it later."

"Can I come?"

Harris jumped in.

"Absolutely not, Michele. You can sit in on our discussions, but you can't do anything at all outside this apartment."

"Why not?"

"These are not nice people we are dealing with. It's too risky for you." Elliott added. Michele pouted but didn't argue. Max quickly changed the subject.

"When I spoke with Zannie yesterday, she was trying to figure out how to follow the money. She says it's the only way we can make sure that everybody gets swept up by the DEA when they make their move."

"I get why," Elliott said then continued. "But it's not going to be easy."

"Right. The drone follows the guys who pick up the protection money, but we don't know for sure which stop they make over the next day is the one where they leave the money they collect", Max said as they all picked up a slice of pizza and began to eat.

"Since it looks like, so far anyway, that there is no one central place that they all go, we're not certain where it's left and where it goes next."

They all ate in silence for a minute before Michele spoke.

"Why don't you put some of that secret gel on the money that the owner of La Hacienda gives to the bad guys?"

They all looked at each other. Elliott was the first to answer.

"Hmm. Good idea Michele."

"Is it?" she asked, beaming at the praise. They all looked at Max and he nodded.

"I'll call Zannie and ask her what she thinks."

"Can you tell her it was my idea?" Michele asked.

Harris shook his head as he replied.

"Now Michele. You know we agreed that you could join us but not tell anyone else you're involved."

She sulked for a moment that looked up.

"How about after it's all over?"

"We'll see."

"OK. Cool," she replied and they all went back to their pizza, Michele managing to hum a tune while she ate hers.

CHAPTER 25

LA HACIENDA

SAN ANTONIO, TEXAS

"She won't do it."

Max looked up from his dinner at the waitress standing beside his table. He had sent her to speak with Consuela about giving her the money for her payments this evening. The group had decided not to tell her it was marked and could be traced. Instead they decided to go for a 'charitable donation' from an admiring customer.

"Why not?" he asked.

The waitress shrugged.

"She didn't say."

"What do you suggest I do?"

She eyed him carefully.

"Why are you offering to do this?"

Max shrugged.

"I caused her a lot of trouble before."

The waitress nodded her head.

"For sure. That's why she doesn't want anything to do with you."

Max sighed. The 'money drone' was already up and waiting to track the money. But first they had to get the marked money into the hands of the bag men. Time to go to plan B.

"OK. I understand. Thanks for trying for me."

"Sure," she replied and moved on to another table.

Max finished his dinner and asked for the check. When the waitress brought it, he glanced at it and put a hundred dollar bill on top of the check.

"You have anything smaller? Your bill's less than twenty dollars," the waitress observed.

"No. Sorry," Max replied, then added "just give me sixty back. Keep the rest as a tip."

She quickly calculated a tip of over twenty dollars and smiled.

"Thanks."

"My pleasure."

Max watched her as she walked to the register, rang up the exchange and returned with his change.

"Here you go. Thanks again," she said. Max just smiled at her. As she walked away he wondered what the odds were that the hundred he just passed on would be used by Consuela later in the evening to pay one of the bag men. He shrugged and got up. He'd know later tonight. If it didn't work they'd have to try some other way of getting marked money into the bad guy's hands, maybe via the drug dealers. He noticed that the waitress watched him as he walked out. He idly wondered how tight she was with the dish washer. Maybe he would agree to use some of the marked money for his next buy.

CHAPTER 26

THE BARRIO

SAN ANTONIO, TEXAS

Elliott sat in his non-descript Toyota a block away from the drug exchange site. He watched through binoculars as Jose, a young man on his payroll, drove up to the stop sign and waited for one of the young boys to run up to the driver's side window. Jose spoke to the boy, the boy replied and a few seconds later Jose passed money out the window to the boy.

The boy trotted to a decrepit building and disappeared inside, and Jose pulled away, turned right and then right again, ending up behind the same building. A different boy, slightly older than the one who took the money strolled out of the building and up to Jose's window. Words were exchanged and the boy handed Jose a package. He then returned to the building as Jose drove away.

Elliott's phone chirped and he tapped a button on it.

"Done," Jose said.

"Good. Any problems?"

"The kid collecting the money wanted to know how I had heard about the location. I told him I heard from a friend who knew a guy who bought there."

"OK. Good job."

"Thanks. Now what?"

"That's it for this job. Get back on the stake out on the Guantino case."

"OK."

Elliott clicked off, searched through his contact list and tapped Max's number. Max answered on the first ring.

"So?"

"It went fine. What about you?"

Max looked out the window of the beat up Blazer he had bought earlier in the day just for this job. He was pretty sure someone in the drug chain he was going to tap into would recognize his rental car, so they had decided he should get a used car.

"I'm about fourth in line right now."

"Just be careful what you say."

"I got it. Don't worry."

Within minutes it was his turn. He buzzed down his window as a teen-aged boy walked up.

"Hey," Max said. The boy just stared at him.

"I was told I could get some stuff here."

"By who?" the boy replied, studying Max as he talked.

Max shrugged.

"Friend a' mine. He told me not to say his name, you know."

Max studied the boy while he was staring back at him. He guessed he was around thirteen or so. He was skinny, medium height and very black. He finally spoke.

"What you want."

"Some ecstasy."

"How much?"

Max held out two one hundred dollar bills.

"As much as this will buy."

"How I know you not a cop?"

Max snorted.

"That'll be the day," he said and held the boy's stare. Finally the boy nodded, snatched the money from Max's hand and stepped back.

"Drive around the block. Stop at the fourth house down on the right and wait."

"Got it," Max said but the boy had already turned away and was jogging toward the worst house on the street, which was saying a lot. He put the Blazer in gear, turned right and then right again. He counted until he was in front of the fourth house and stopped. Nothing happened for a minute or so, and then Max saw a rustling at the dirty curtain hanging in one of the windows. A few seconds later the door opened and a different boy came out and walked slowly to the Blazer, looking back and forth as he came.

When he arrived at the Blazer he looked both ways up and down the street and then held out a small paper bag.

Max reached for it and the boy held on to it for another second before letting go.

"Thanks," Max said but the boy just turned away and went back into the house. Max put the car in gear and pulled away, not seeing the man sitting behind the curtain in the house watching him. The man that he had hit first in the kitchen at La Hacienda. He also didn't notice the white van that turned the corner and followed him down the street.

CHAPTER 27

STREETS

SAN ANTONIO

Max was working his way back to Harris's apartment when his phone buzzed. He picked it up and tapped the answer icon.

"What's up Elliott?"

"You're being followed."

Max glanced in his rear view mirror and scanned the cars behind him.

"Which one?"

"The white van picked you up as you left your buy."

"You were following me?"

"I had someone on you, yeah."

Max paused before replying.

"Thanks. I should have been watching."

"Hey, no worries. What do you want to do?"

Max thought through his options before replying.

"It's probably best if I lose them rather than confronting them, don't you think?"

There was a pause as Elliott also considered their options.

"I can't think of a good reason to engage. Not right now, anyway. It would just get them more alert."

"Why do you think they're following me?"

"Either they follow every new buyer or somebody recognized you."

"Yeah, probably the latter."

"Then its not a good idea to whack the nest again."

"Agreed. So, how do I lose them?"

"How badly do you need that piece of crap you're driving?"

Max smiled.

"What's your plan?"

"Drive to the airport, park in long term parking and take the shuttle to the terminal. Go in at the first stop and walk through to the far end. Get a cab to the Hyatt. Go in the front, through the lobby and out to the pool in the back. There's a gate there to the parking lot. I'll meet you there."

"Got it."

Max cut the phone line and glanced at the van still following. He smiled to himself.

"Here we go, boys. Let's have some fun."

He opened *waze* and set the airport as his destination.

CHAPTER 28

HARRIS HOME

SAN ANTONIO, TEXAS

"So, are you sure the guys didn't follow me?" Max asked, still a little irritated that he had allowed himself to be followed in the first place.

"Positive," Elliott replied.

"How can you be sure? They could have followed the bus to the terminal, and when they saw me get off, the passenger could have jumped out and followed me through the terminal, then followed."

Elliott held up a hand stopping him.

"Didn't happen," Elliott said, shaking his head.

"But how do you know?" Max started and stopped when Elliott gave him a sharp look.

"They had an accident."

"What?"

"They ran into one of my people, literally."

Max's face scrunched up.

"How many people do you have working for you?"

"Just enough," Elliott replied with a small smile.

Harris cleared his throat and interjected himself into the conversation.

"We seem to have been successful in inserting marked money into the system," he said and pointed to the open computer.

"We're showing four different lines; one from the Mexican group of protection money, one of the same from the mafia, and one each from the drug sales of each group."

He spun the computer around so Elliott and Max could see the screen. Four different colored dots appeared on the screen, with three of the colors grouping together tightly on two spots.

"Looks like we can identify the clearing houses for both groups," Max said.

"And the fourth color is the one you just put into play by buying the drugs. It should show up at the Mafia center soon."

"When do you think the money will be showing up in banks?" Harris asked and Elliott answered.

"They probably make regular deposits, say every other day or so."

Just as he said it the two colors belonging to the Mexican group appeared at a new location. Harris tapped the screen and words appeared next to the two dots.

ODESSA NATIONAL BANK

"There you go," Elliott said, excitement in his voice.

"From here on the DEA guys will have to follow the money. The computer geeks won't be able to help," Harris said. They settled into a quiet time, talking softly about when to get the DEA involved. Suddenly the computer sounded a ding and Elliott peered at the writing on the screen.

"Maybe the DEA won't have too much trouble following the money," Elliott said as more writing began to appear on the screen just below the name of the bank.

$1.6 MILLION TRANSFERRED TO

NATIONAL BANK OF THE VIRGIN ISLANDS

$.9 MILLION TRANSFERRED TO VBI BANK

"How can they know that?" Elliott asked.

"They probably hacked into the banks computers," Max said, shaking his head.

Elliott also shook his head.

"Seems to be some pretty talented criminals in our University system," Elliott replied.

"Glad they're on our side," was all Harris said, and the other two men just nodded their heads.

CHAPTER 29

HARRIS'S OFFICE

SAN ANTONIO, TEXAS

"How did you get all of this information?" the DEA lawyer was shaking his head as he studied the charts and the lists of names, addresses, specific crimes, bank names and amounts transferred. No one answered and he looked up and stared at each man in turn, Harris, then Elliott and finally Max.

"Well" he prodded.

Max cleared his throat.

"I asked for help with a problem I was having here."

The DEA lawyer, David Murphy nodded.

"Yeah, I heard about that. You attacked two guys in a restaurant. I read the police report."

Max colored slightly.

"That's not how it came down. The two guys were muscling the owner, trying to get her to pay protection money. I," he paused, shrugged and continued. "I just stepped in and stopped them."

"Not how the report reads," Murphy countered.

"That's why we got into all of this in the first place, Dave," Harris interjected and then turned back to Max, encouraging him to continue.

"Anyway, I contacted a friend of mine, a student at Cornell. He came up with the drone idea to follow the guys who do the collecting. And then the drug guys, and finally the money. Another student there, a grad student in Math, I think, did the actual programming."

"And they're the ones who tapped into the banks computers?"

Max nodded, knowing Murphy was upset.

"You do realize we can't use any of that information. It was obtained illegally."

"But, you've got everyone involved. Once you suspect them of the crimes, you can get a warrant to go to the banks and ask them to follow the money." Harris jumped in.

"Maybe," was all Murphy said. He studied the information again and looked up at Harris.

"The local police aren't going to come out of this looking to good."

"Agreed," Harris said.

"And that'll probably rub off on you."

Harris nodded again, and Max jumped in.

"He's ready to go out on his own. Maybe he can start somewhere else." He hesitated and then continued.

"Maybe you can help with that too."

"Too?" Murphy glared at Max.

"Yeah," Harris plunged in. "You know, we want you to get the charges against Max tossed out."

Murphy closed the file and stood up.

"I need to take this information with me."

Harris looked concerned.

"You're going to move on this, right?"

Murphy looked at Harris for a long moment.

"It's my guess that the investigators will go bat shit over this. My guess is it'll make the careers for a lot of guys."

Everyone smiled until he continued.

"But, let's see. I've been wrong before. And I have no idea if they'll be willing to deal at all, or if they'll just confiscate everything and run with it on their own."

"And not help Max?" Harris asked.

Murphy ignored the question and took a step toward the door.

"I'll get back to you."

"When?" Harris asked.

"When I know more."

Murphy nodded and walked out the door, leaving the rest of them staring forlornly at the space he had just occupied.

CHAPTER 30

HARRIS'S OFFICE

SAN ANTONIO, TEXAS

Three days had passed with no word from Murphy, or anyone else at the DEA. Max was trying to remain calm, but wasn't doing so well at it. He was sitting in the small conference room working on his fifth cup of coffee when Elliott entered the room.

"Hey. Any word?" he asked. Max just shook his head.

"Where's Sing?"

"He's at the court house. Got called down there by a judge."

"What about?"

"Didn't say. Don't think he knew what it was about."

Elliott nodded, walked to the sideboard and poured his own cup of coffee. He returned to the table and took a seat across from Max. They drank in silence for a few minutes and then the door flew open and Harris rushed in. They both almost jumped out of their seats. Harris hurried in, threw himself into a chair, dropped his battered briefcase on the desk and opened it.

"What's up?" Elliott asked. Harris held up his hand calling for no interruptions. Elliott and Max watched him pull out a file, place it on the desk and open it. He glanced at both of them and began.

"OK. Here's the deal."

"From who?" Elliott asked and Harris shot him a look. Elliott held up his hands and leaned back. Harris continued.

"The DEA wants to run with everything." Max broke into a smile and Harris held up a hand again.

"That's the good news. Actually, not all of the good news. They'll also take care of your charges. They'll all be dropped and the record expunged."

"But?" Elliott interjected.

"But, they want to be the stars of the show."

"Which means?"

"Which means they'll confiscate the drones and all of the information. Neither Zeke nor Zannie gets credit for anything. Neither does Cornell."

Max slumped at the words.

"But that's' not fair!" he said.

"Seriously? You expect *fair* from the government?" Harris answered.

"Did you agree?" Elliott asked.

"Of course not. I told them I'd have to talk to Zeke, Zannie and Cornell."

"And they said?"

"It's Thursday. They said they'd give me until the week end. On Monday morning they're going to start picking up the suspects, whether the Cornell people agree or not."

"Great," Max said in disgust.

"What are you going to do?" Harris asked.

Max sighed.

"I'll have to call Zeke and Zannie and tell them what's going on."

"And then?" Elliott asked.

Max thought about it for a moment and then smiled.

"And then I'm going to get out of the way before they strike back."

CHAPTER 31

HARRIS'S OFFICE

SAN ANTONIO, TEXAS

"Well," Harris said to the other two men, "it's Sunday afternoon. Tomorrow morning the DEA plans to confiscate all the hardware, software and information. Did you get anywhere with the people at Cornell."

Max glanced at Elliott before answering. He tried to keep from smiling.

"Let's call the group Cornell, since that's what's at the top of the hill there."

"OK," Harris said and Max continued.

"Cornell suggests that you tell the DEA that they will be happy to work together with the DEA. Cornell will maintain ownership of the drones and will work closely with the DEA tech guys in collecting and analyzing data. The DEA can be in total charge of the actual field work and dealing with the media. All Cornell wants is for the DEA to acknowledge that Cornell is working with them to gather the data."

Harris shrugged.

"Why would the DEA agree to that? They're the government. They can do whatever they want."

"True," Max nodded. "But they should be reminded that the programmers working on this project at Cornell are remarkably resourceful."

"So?" Elliott jumped in. "Who cares?" Harris nodded his agreement. Max smiled, opened a folder and pulled out a dozen sheets of paper. He flipped through them before selecting two and sliding them across the table to Harris.

"Joseph Wilkerson. Head of the DEA. He would probably be interested in the information on these two sheets of paper."

Harris picked up the first page and began to read. Before long his eyes grew big. He stopped reading and looked at Max.

"Is this information real?"

Max just nodded as Harris slid the paper to Elliott who had the same response as Harris.

"Seriously?" he asked.

"That's what they tell me."

"This is all extremely confidential information," Harris said and Elliott agreed and read some of the top lines.

"Bank accounts, including balances. Stock owned. List of credit cards, their numbers and recent charges. Real estate holdings." He paused and looked at Max, who responded.

"Their point is, they are the best at hacking. If the DEA closes them out of the picture, who knows where this info might show up?"

"But that's illegal as hell, isn't it!" Elliott asked.

"Please, Elliott. These guys are so good that the DEA will never be able to pin anything on them," Max shot back.

"And those other sheets of paper?" Harris asked, pointing to the papers still in front of Max.

"The rest of the top management at the DEA."

Harris sat back and rolled his eyes.

"Guess I'd better get on the phone with Murphy, ASAP."

"Good idea," Max replied and watched as Harris scooped up the papers and left the room.

CHAPTER 32

ELLIOTT'S OFFICE

SAN ANTONIO, TEXAS

Elliott was sitting at his desk when his secretary called through from her small front office.

"Mister Walker is here," her soft voice purred. Elliott leaned forward and toggled the intercom switch.

"Please send him in, Georgia."

Seconds later Max swept into the room holding a cup of Starbucks coffee and carrying a Dunkin' Donuts box. He placed the box on Elliott's desk and sat in one of the two visitor chairs.

"You could have gotten coffee here for free," Elliott chided. Max nodded.

"Yeah, I know. I've had some of your coffee."

"Ouch," Elliott said and then smiled. "Don't let Georgia hear you say that."

"Heard from Sing yet?" Max asked after a sip of coffee and a bite from a chocolate frosted donut.

"He called about ten minutes ago. He's on his way."

"Great. Any indication of how it went?"

"He sounded, uh, harassed."

Max just nodded and the two men lapsed into silence, each searching his thoughts, trying to guess the outcome of the Harris – Murphy meetings. Five minutes later Georgia announced his arrival and Harris burst through the door.

"Hey, guys," he said as he dropped into the vacant chair and grabbed a donut, setting his briefcase on the floor by his feet. Max only waited a few seconds before anxiously asking, "So?"

Harris paused long enough to sip from the cup Georgia handed him before answering.

"Murphy was really pissed when I laid the threat on him. Ranted, raved, and threatened to arrest everyone involved. You know the drill."

"And then?" Elliott prodded. Harris looked at Max as he replied.

"Your pals are amazing."

"Why? What happened?" Max replied.

"While he's ranting and raving his computer pings the arrival of an email. He stops, opens the email and turns a whiter shade of pale, as the old song went."

"What was in the email?" Elliott asked.

"Every detail you could think of relating to Mister Murphy's financial affairs."

Max grinned and shook his head in admiration.

"Perfect timing."

"How did they know you were in a meeting with him?" Elliott asked.

Harris shrugged.

"My guess is they put some gel on me."

"How did he react?" Max asked.

"He went ballistic, and ended up calling in one of the DEA's computer geeks. Wanted him to trace the email back to see where it came from."

"And?"

"You're going to love this. They set it up so the email looked like it came from the head of the DEA, and the head of the FBI was copied."

"Awesome," Max said, smiling.

"Yeah. That got the FBI involved. The DEA will collect all the drug dealers and the FBI will get the numbers runners, the prostitution rings and the protection rackets.

And then?" Elliott asked.

"They all eventually caved. The DEA and the FBI will run everything but Cornell will be given credit for developing the system and your two people will be offered very lucrative jobs with the DEA as consultants."

"That's awesome," Elliott said shaking his head. Harris nodded and looked at Max.

"And, I just came from the judge's chambers. You're free. All charges dropped." Max looked at Elliott.

"You have anything stronger than coffee in the office? Seems like we need to celebrate."

CHAPTER 33

RV PARK

SAN ANTONIO, TEXAS

Max had spent most of the morning on the phone with Zannie, Zeke and several representatives from Cornell. It seemed to him that everyone there was OK with the setup with the DEA, which made him very happy. The DEA had already started a series of massive raids, gathering up a huge number of drug dealers, protection thugs and their bosses.

Max now had a map out on his kitchen table, trying to decide where he wanted to stop on his trek toward California. His phone rang and he glanced at the caller ID.

The name **PER WAHL** stared back at him and a shudder of concern ran through him. Was something wrong with Steven? He grabbed the phone and hit ANSWER.

"Max?" came the strong voice of the Captain of one of the largest research ships in the world.

"Hey, Per. What's up?" Max tried to keep the concern out of his voice.

"I've just been reassigned."

"Ah! Is that good news?"

"It's what it is. The captain of *Seaquest,* a research vessel working off the coast of Baja, has fallen ill, and I've been ordered to replace him and bring his ship to port."

Max wasn't sure what he should say next, and Wahl helped him out.

"I'm telling you this because I'm taking Steven with me, and we expect to arrive in port somewhere in Baja, Mexico next week. I thought you might want to meet us there."

Max's throat tightened.

"That's very nice of you to think of me, Per. I'd be glad to meet the ship. Do you know where yet?"

"No. I'll have to assess the situation first. I can text you when I decide the destination and arrival date."

"Great. How's Steven doing?"

"He's got a real gift for this work. You can be very proud of your son."

"Thanks Per. Thanks for everything."

"No problem. You'll hear from me by the end of the week."

They said their good byes and Max went back to the map, planning a route to the western most state of Mexico. He sat back and talked out loud to himself.

"End of the week? I have time for one last meal at La Hacienda before leave." He smiled at the thought and set about preparing for his next adventure.

www.ingramcontent.com/pod-product-compliance
Lightning Source LLC
Chambersburg PA
CBHW070912160726
48004CB00003B/1342